Disney's
Winnie the Pooh
Sharing Can Be Fun

Sharing things

With all your friends

Can be a lot of fun!

For when you share,

It brings a smile

To you and everyone!

One very hot day in the Hundred-Acre Wood, Piglet and Pooh went walking in search of a chilly spot. As they walked, they tried everything they could think of to cool off.

First they ran up and down hoping to catch a breeze. But that
just made them hotter. Then Pooh climbed a tree, hoping the
wind would blow through the branches. But it didn't.

"I have an idea," Pooh yelled down to Piglet.

Pooh pointed at the stream in the distance. "Perhaps we could find a log and float away to someplace cooler."
"Oh, Pooh," said Piglet. "That's a wonderful idea!"

So Pooh and Piglet started toward the stream. Rounding the first bend, they met Eeyore standing in the path.

"Come with us to cool off," cried Piglet. "We're going to make a log ride and float away."

And so the three friends continued through the Wood.
"Where are you going?" called Owl from above.
"To the stream," cried Piglet. "We're going to make a log
ride and float away."

"Splendid idea!" said Owl. "May I join you?"

"Of course," replied Pooh. And after going just a little farther, the four friends reached the stream at last.

Eeyore looked around. "There are four of us," he said.
"Yes, we know," Owl replied.
"It'll never work," Eeyore said.
"Why not?" asked Piglet.

"Too many of us," Eeyore explained, "unless we find the perfect log."

"It must be long enough for all of us to sit on, but short enough for us to steer," Owl said.

"Perhaps we should have a contest. The first one to find the perfect log gets to sit in front!" cried Piglet as he started off into the Wood with Pooh.

But finding the right-size log wasn't so easy. Pooh found a log that was way too long. Piglet found a log that was far too short. And Eeyore found no logs at all, just lots of thistles.

"Oh, bother," said Pooh. "Perhaps it wasn't such a splendid idea after all."

"Wait!" cried Piglet. "Rabbit's got it!" he said, pointing.

And sure enough, along came Rabbit, rolling the perfect log. "We're making a log ride to float down the stream," Piglet explained. "We've looked and looked for just the right log. And you have gone and found it!"

"Absolutely not!" said Rabbit. "I spent this long, hot morning looking for just the right log for my garden. And now that I've found it, it's mine."

"But don't you want to share?" asked Piglet in a little voice.

"But this log is for my garden," said Rabbit, "for under my tree, so I can sit in the shade."

"How about just one very little ride?" asked Piglet.

"Doesn't matter much anyway," Eeyore said.
"There!" cried Rabbit. "Just listen to Eeyore. It doesn't matter."
"If we all go for a ride, you can sit in front," offered Pooh.
"All right!" cried Rabbit. "Take the log. But you only get one ride!"

"And then you have to help me push the log all the way to my garden," added Rabbit.

After agreeing to help Rabbit, the friends set the log in the stream and hopped on.

"Whee!" they cried as they floated down the stream. Rabbit sat in front, followed by Pooh and Piglet, Eeyore and Owl. The friends splashed and sploshed and laughed and giggled. Everyone looked happy—even Rabbit.

"That was wonderful," said Piglet as they came to a stop at the end of the stream. "Let's do it again!"

"Oh, no, you don't," declared Rabbit. "I said *one* time, and I meant it. Now the log goes up to my garden."

No one was happy about it, but a promise was a promise. So Eeyore, Owl, Piglet, and Pooh all helped Rabbit push the log into his garden.

Rabbit stood back to admire his log. "A perfect fit," he said.

"The perfect fit," repeated Owl glumly.

"Oh, bother. Guess we'll go now," said Pooh softly.

As Rabbit watched his friends walk away, he thought about how sad they all looked. He began to feel very sad, too.

Suddenly Rabbit had an idea.
Running after his friends, he called out, "Wait! Stop—er—anyone want to share a log?"

"The way I look at it," said Rabbit, "if I use the log, it's just for me. But if I share my log, then you feel good, too. And that makes me feel even better."

And so the five friends carried Rabbit's log back to the stream. And they floated...and floated...and floated. Rabbit sat in front because, after all, it was his log.

The sun was beginning to set as the friends rode down the stream for the very last time.

"Let's put the log back in Rabbit's garden," said Piglet as they came to a stop.

"I have a better idea," said Rabbit. "Let's leave it here so we can ride it again tomorrow. I had no idea that sharing could be so much fun."

A LESSON A DAY
POOH'S WAY

Good things happen

when you share.